THIS BOOK BELONGS TO

D1409283

DAUGHTER
OF THE
GREAT ZANDINI

DAUGHTER
OF THE
GREAT ZANDINI

Cary Fagan

Illustrated by Cybèle Young

Tundra Books

Text copyright © 2001 by Cary Fagan
Illustrations copyright © 2001 by Cybèle Young

Published in Canada by Tundra Books,
481 University Avenue, Toronto, Ontario M5G 2E9

Published in the United States by Tundra Books of Northern New York,
P.O. Box 1030, Plattsburgh, New York 12901

Library of Congress Card Number: 2001086829

National Library of Canada Cataloguing in Publication Data

Fagan, Cary
    Daughter of the Great Zandini

ISBN 0-88776-534-3

I. Young, Cybèle, 1972- . II. Title.

PS8561.A375D38 2001   jC813'.54   C2001-930263-0
PZ7.F33Da 2001

We acknowledge the support of the Canada Council for the Arts and the Ontario
Arts Council for our publishing program.

We acknowledge the financial support of the Government of Canada through the
Book Publishing Industry Development Program for our publishing activities.

Design: Ingrid Paulson
Medium: pen and ink
Printed in Canada

1 2 3 4 5 6   06 05 04 03 02 01

For Rachel, my partner in magic
C. F.

For the Mighty Jidoo
C. Y.

* 1 *

FATHER MAKES AN ANNOUNCEMENT

At dinner one evening, I was trying to make a pencil rise from my hand when Father suddenly banged his palm on the table. "What's this?" he cried. He had been glancing at the newspaper while we waited for Matilda to bring in the meal and now he slapped the paper in disgust. "Of course," he said. "Besette!"

I knew who Besette was – A. S. Besette, the notorious journalist who wrote for the *Gazette*, the most powerful newspaper in Paris. Since even before I was born, he and my father had been enemies. Now father pulled at his mustache, which he always did when he was angry.

"What does it say in the paper?" asked my brother Theodore, running his hand dreamily through his hair. Not long ago, Theo had worn short pants like all the other boys, but just last month Father had taken him to the tailor for his first suit. I was jealous; my father made me wear sailor dresses and other frilly frocks for young girls. "Read it to us, Papa," he said.

"All right, I will," said Father, straightening his stiff collar, for even at home he dressed formally. "You ought to know just what that scoundrel is putting into print for everyone to see." He began to read the article aloud in his most scornful voice.

ZANDINI A WASH-UP?

BY A. S. BESETTE, CONJURING REPORTER

It has been over a year since the Great Zandini, whom many consider to be the world's finest magician, last performed on a stage in our great city. True, that show was an enormous success, but since then not a word has been heard of the conjurer. Could it be that Zandini's days as a performer are over? Is he too old? Is he all washed up? And what of his son? Will he continue the Zandini family tradition and take his father's place on stage? Or will he prove a failure like his uncle Zachariah, who disappeared so many years ago and is rumored to be working as a small-time circus performer in South America? Perhaps young Theodore has also failed to inherit the talent of his father, grandfather, and great-grandfather. If so, then the name Zandini will soon be forgotten.

Father stood up and raised the newspaper over his head. "Forgotten!" he roared. "You hear that?" At that moment, the newspaper burst into flames as if from the heat of father's anger. Unfortunately, just then Matilda entered from the kitchen with a large platter in her hands. "Heaven help us!" she shrieked, dropping the platter onto the table.

"Forgive me, Matilda," Father said, dousing the flames into the water pitcher on the table. "My emotions got away from me. I do not mean to spoil the fine meal you have prepared." Calm again, he lifted the silver lid from the platter, only to uncover a live goose, which raised its head and honked. Matilda screamed and ran back into the kitchen. Well, she had only been with us a week and still wasn't used to our ways. In our household, housekeepers did not usually last very long.

"How inconvenient," Father said and winked at my brother and me, his good humor having returned. He put the lid down again and picked it up to reveal a roasted duck surrounded by potatoes. Of course Theodore and I were not surprised. After all, our father *was* the Great Zandini.

"Papa," I said, "How can that terrible A. S. Besette write such things?"

"For years now he has tried to destroy my reputation and my career. But to mention my brother is going too far. That ink-stained wretch knows just how to wound me. But even I must admit that Besette is right about one thing: it is time that I take to the stage once again. My devoted admirers have waited long enough. I shall dazzle

them with a new show of even more astonishing feats. Yes, I will present magical illusions the likes of which Paris has never seen before. Transformations, alterations, manipulations, penetrations, levitations . . ."

Listening to Father, I became so excited that I dropped the pencil from my hand. It clattered under the table and rolled toward Father's feet.

"Fanny, I've told you a hundred times not to practice during dinner."

"But Papa, you say that a magician must always be practicing."

"So I do," he sighed, reaching down for the pencil. Absentmindedly, he made it disappear into his ear. "You might tell that to your brother. Are you listening, Theodore?"

As usual, my brother was gazing out the window at the carriages going by and, beyond them, a boat drifting along the River Seine. I

saw that he had arranged the peas on his plate in the shape of the letter 'C'. Of course! He was thinking about Colette, the girl who lived in the next apartment. He was *always* thinking about Colette. I couldn't imagine anything duller.

"Theodore!" Father said with impatience.

"Yes, Papa?"

"This will be no ordinary show, Theo. The truth is I *am* getting older. It's time for the Great Zandini to present his son and successor, the next in line of the Zandini dynasty."

Father swept his arm toward the portraits in oval frames along the dining room wall: Great-grandfather, then Grandfather, then Father himself – the great line of magicians. On the same wall was a painting of my late mother, beneath which my father put a fresh rose in a vase each day. And in the corner, hidden by a plant on top of a bookcase, was one of Uncle Zachariah, whose name was not to be spoken in the house.

"It's time, Theo," Father said, "for you to appear on stage with me."

"But Papa, couldn't I just assist behind the scenes?"

Our father was a good man, but he did sometimes have a temper. Now he brought his hand down on his wine glass – *smack!* Fortunately, the glass vanished.

"Nonsense," he said. "Tomorrow we begin rehearsing."

* 2 *

PRACTICE, PRACTICE, PRACTICE

In the morning, Father hired a carriage to take us to the theater. It was a warm summer day, school was over, and all of Paris was out on the boulevards, strolling arm in arm, walking dogs, riding bicycles. Naturally everyone recognized the Great Zandini as he went by. Men raised their straw boaters to us while women waved from under their parasols. Children stopped rolling their hoops or pulling wooden trains to stare in wonder at the famous magician. Even the tram drivers clanged their bells.

Now, Paris was a city of entertainment. There was the great opera house, there were theaters for comedies and bloody tragedies, for orchestras and ballets, for performing acrobats and horses, even theaters that filled with water for swimmers. There was a panorama, where, for just a franc, you could go up a stairway and see a single painting all around you showing a tremendous battle scene. There were horse races and circuses and marionette shows and masked balls

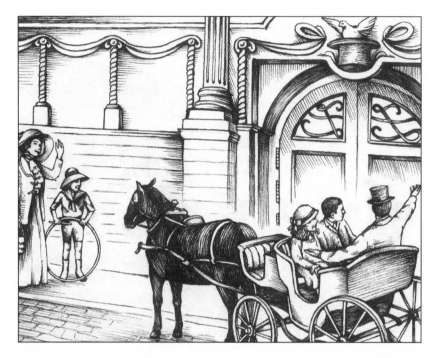

that went from midnight to dawn. What *wasn't* there in Paris? But the most exciting place that I knew was the Theater Zandini, and as we pulled up to it my heart soared like the dove rising from the upturned hat that was carved in stone over the doors.

As we stepped down from the carriage, the doorman made a deep bow and opened the door. "Monsieur Zandini," he said, "you do us a great honor by returning to the theater." My father nodded gracefully, threw his cape over his shoulder, and walked in as if returning home after a long absence.

To me the theater always felt strange when it was empty, as if it were not quite real or were perhaps sleeping until the people came to fill its velvet seats. I sat alone in the front row while Father stood on the stage and delivered a lecture to Theodore in the same deep and resounding voice that he used during a performance.

"Remember, son, that conjuring is an honorable tradition going back to ancient times. We do not pretend to be witches or sorcerers but artists who can astonish and delight with our illusions. For a little while we can make people believe in the unbelievable. We can make the impossible seem possible. We turn reason upside down. And why do people care for this peculiar talent of ours? Because they want to believe that wonderful and surprising things might indeed happen, even to them. And because they know that the world is not always as it seems. No, it is full of mystery. Theodore, are you paying attention?"

My brother was gently stroking a lock of Colette's hair, which he kept in a little silver case in his breast pocket. She had snipped off the curl for him only last week, and he carried it wherever he went. I, however, heard every word my father spoke. I loved this talent of my family's and hungered for it to be my own.

Father continued. "First, Theodore, you must practice. A mastery of sleight of hand is essential. You must be able to perform movements that at first seem awkward or unnatural, but that in time will become second nature. Next, you must develop confidence. A commanding air on the stage rivets the attention of the audience. If you are not in control at all times – disaster! All right, let's begin."

Working up my courage, I called to Father from my seat. "Papa, what about me? What am I going to do in the show?"

My voice sounded small in the theater. Father looked at me kindly from the stage. "You, Fanny? Let me think. You are just about the right size for the Indian Basket illusion. We will put you into the basket, close the lid, and thrust in a dozen swords. Won't that be fun?"

In the afternoon, Father had to arrange for posters to be printed for the new show, so Theodore did not have to rehearse. He went for a walk with Colette in the Tuileries Gardens, giving me strict instructions to stay ten paces behind them. Instead of being silent and dreamy, now he talked excitedly, picked up a smooth stone to show her, jumped about with energy. Colette had so many frills and bows on her dress that I didn't know how she could move. For the life of me, I couldn't understand what made her so fascinating to my brother, as she knew no riddles, wasn't interested in balancing on ledges or catching fireflies in jars, and worst of all, didn't like magic. Still, Theo adored Colette, so I *tried* to be nice to her.

Only after he had taken her home again would my brother walk with me along the riverbank. A painter had set up his easel while, on the other side of the river, an organ-grinder was turning the handle of her instrument. My brother didn't notice any of them; he was too miserable. I tried to cheer him up by plucking toffees from behind his ears.

"Please stop," Theodore said. "You are only reminding me of how badly I am failing Papa."

"But dear Theodore," I cried. "What's the matter? This is your great chance."

I followed him onto the bridge. Theodore stopped to look down at the water. "It's not a great chance if a person doesn't care for it. I don't want to be a magician."

"You don't?"

"Fanny, every day after school for the last year Father has been trying to teach me the basics of magic. We stand in the parlor and he shows me the French Drop, or a False Shuffle, or the Classic Palm. How can I remember them all? Even worse, I'm clumsy. I can't get the coins and cards and balls to do what they are supposed to. They tumble to the floor while my fingers end up in knots. You're different, Fanny. I've seen how you watch from the doorway and then try it yourself. For you magic comes naturally. Maybe if I really wanted to perform and be famous it would be different. But I don't like the idea of being on the stage with everybody staring goggle-eyed at me."

I looked at my brother in amazement. How could one person love something and another feel the very opposite? Father was right; the world really was full of mystery. I took Theodore's hand. "Then tell me, Theo, what does make you happy?"

"Phonographs."

"Phonographs?"

"The new machines that make music in your home. I want to open a shop when I'm old enough and wear a brown suit and sell recordings of marching bands and orchestras and the latest popular songs. I want to marry Colette and have six children and take them for a stroll in the gardens on Sunday afternoons."

"You want to do that instead of becoming a magician?"

"Yes," Theodore said with a sigh.

I sighed too. "You will just have to tell Papa."

"No, Fanny. I can't disappoint him. He is counting on me to be the next Great Zandini. You must help me to be resigned to my fate and to become a better magician."

He dropped the stone into the water.

* 3 *

MAGICIANS IN THE FAMILY

Every day for a month I watched Father and Theodore rehearse. It was painful to see Theodore looking so lost on the stage. He stood unnaturally still or made sudden and disconcerting motions, and when he walked from one side to the other his legs moved as stiffly as a wooden soldier's. And his voice! It came out as a squeak. "From the diaphragm! Speak from the diaphragm!" shouted my father, but poor Theo's voice only grew smaller.

And yet Father insisted that Theo was improving every day, his illusions becoming more believable and his stage presence more appealing. Did Father really believe this or was he just trying to encourage Theo? Perhaps the truth lay in the fact that instead of performing half the show, Father decided that Theo should "get his feet wet" by doing only one illusion each night. "You see, son," he said. "The show is coming together just as I said it would. You just need to look as if you are enjoying yourself."

It was true. On stage, Theodore looked as if he were about to face a firing squad. Theodore answered meekly, "Yes, Papa, I'll try."

Matters were not made better by an article that appeared one morning in the *Gazette*.

GREAT ZANDINI TAKES STAGE AGAIN

BY A. S. BESETTE, CONJURING REPORTER

News that the Great Zandini is preparing a new show to open next month has galloped across Paris. Can it be that this humble reporter has shamed the conjurer into proving that he still has what it takes to bring in an audience? Perhaps this time Parisians will find that the old magician's musty bag of tricks leaves them yawning. Word has it that Zandini Junior will also perform, but whether young Theodore can prove that he has inherited the family talent has yet to be seen. That is the question that this reporter looks forward to answering for his readers.

"Musty bag of tricks?" Father roared. "That Besette! Why, I'll make him disappear! I'll turn him into a handful of salt and blow him into the wind!"

For a moment, I think Father wished that he were a real sorcerer.

In the afternoons, Father had much else to arrange. He hired an orchestra to play the music. He supervised the carpenters, painters, and other skilled trades-people as they built new props and sets, as well as special tables, boxes, trunks, and cages whose secrets are known only to conjurers. While he was out, I rehearsed with Theo all over again, first taking the part of Father and then of Theo.

"Look at how much fun you're having," Theo said with annoyance. "You, at least, don't have to pretend you're enjoying yourself."

I frowned, trying to look out of sorts. But Theo was right; each day I looked forward to rehearsing. Was I secretly glad to be better at magic than my older brother? What an awful thought, especially since I loved Theo and wanted him to succeed. I doubled my efforts to make a magician out of him.

One evening Father came in as usual to turn down our lamps and wish us good night. "Papa," I said, "tell me about the family. How we became magicians, I mean."

"Again, Fanny?" He smiled in the darkness. "All right. Come into Theodore's room so he can hear too. It might inspire him."

Theo was sitting up in bed looking through a catalog of phonographs. He quickly slipped it under his pillow while I perched on the end of his bed, tucking my nightgown around me. Father pulled up a chair and began speaking in a quiet voice. "The very first member of the Zander family to be a magician was your great-grandfather Mordecai. He was a cobbler, who traveled with a donkey and a little wagon, stopping in each village square to repair shoes and then moving on again. He had a thick beard and wore a long coat. On Friday afternoons someone would always take him home for the Sabbath meal.

"Well, one day Mordecai hammered new soles on the boots of a bookseller, who asked Mordecai if he would choose a book from his shop as payment. For some reason Mordecai picked up a tattered old pamphlet of conjuring tricks, and the bookseller was only too happy to let him have it. In the evenings Mordecai practiced the tricks. Not long afterwards he came to a village where nobody needed any shoes repaired. Since he had nothing to do, Mordecai set out a little table and put on it three cracked teacups. He turned the teacups upside down and put a button under one of them. When he lifted the cup the button was gone, only to have jumped to another. He made it vanish again and reappear under his hat. He turned it into a lemon."

"That's the Cups and Balls, right Papa? The oldest trick in magic."

"Yes, Fanny. It was even performed in ancient Egypt. But a good trick never grows stale, and the people watching Mordecai clapped and dropped a few coins into one of the cups. After that Mordecai performed at each village he visited. He never smiled or seemed to notice that anyone was watching him."

"Why didn't he ever smile?" I asked.

"I'm not sure. Perhaps he was lonely."

"Tell us how he met Great-grandmother."

"Always in such a hurry, Fanny. All right. In one village a woman with a handkerchief on her head stood among the farmers and merchants, watching. After everyone had drifted away she said to him,

'Why just turn the ball into a lemon? Why not an egg? Or even better, a real baby chick?'

"Mordecai looked up. He said to her, 'Come to my next show.' She did, and sure enough, he turned the button into a live chick. This time he got twice as many coins."

"She was smart," I said.

"That's just what Mordecai thought. So he said to her, 'By any chance are you not yet married?' And that's how the young woman, whose name was Fanny –"

"Just like me!"

"Just like you, became your great-grandmother. Now, in time they had a son, and when the son grew older Mordecai taught him not only the art of cobbling but also the conjuring tricks he knew. Avram, the son, loved performing magic even more than his father did. He found more books and learned more tricks. In larger towns there was sometimes a real magician performing, and Avram paid the magician to teach him."

"But he wasn't satisfied, was he, Papa?"

"No, Fanny, he didn't want to perform only when there was no cobbling work to be done. So one day Avram rented a room with benches in it above a village inn. He pasted handbills about the village square, announcing a conjuring performance by "Zandini" – a name that he thought sounded more like a magician's than Zander. He trimmed his beard, wore a short jacket, and smiled and chatted with the audience. He showed them that a velvet bag was empty and then pulled from it a pair of shoes, a lamp, and a live rooster. He borrowed a woman's scarf, burnt it to ashes, and restored it whole again. And his best illusion – well, for that he asked a young boy to sit on a chair and then covered him with a large blanket. When Avram pulled away the blanket, the chair was empty. And where was the boy? Standing at the very back of the room. And do you know who that boy was?"

Father always asked me that. And I replied as always: "You!"

"That's right. I grew up to become the next magician in the family. And in my turn, I was not satisfied to perform in a room with benches. One day I rented a real theater. Before long the theater was full every night. Soon I was traveling to all the big cities to perform. The newspapers called me the Great Zandini, the most brilliant conjurer of the age."

"And then you met Mother."

"Yes, your dear mother. I was performing here in Paris when she came up to me at the stage door one evening. Why, she asked, did I travel from city to city when I could have my own theater here? 'Everyone visits Paris,' she said. 'Let the people come to you.' And that's just what I did."

"She was smart too."

"Yes, she was."

"But Papa, you never speak of Uncle Zachariah."

Even in the dark I could see Father frown with displeasure. "Now, Fanny . . ."

"I think I am old enough to know, Papa."

He drew his hand over his tired face. "Yes, I suppose so. Zachariah is my older brother. Our father taught both of us to be magicians, and when we were young we performed together. But the simple truth is that I was the better conjurer, and Zachariah resented me. When my father decided to retire, he announced that I was the one who ought to become the next Zandini. For several years, Zachariah worked as my assistant, but he was never happy. One day during a performance he was supposed to appear inside a large dollhouse that had been empty when it was closed up. But when I opened the dollhouse, he wasn't there. He did it to humiliate me on stage. And I never saw Zachariah again."

"Oh, Papa. And is Uncle Zachariah really in South America?"

"South America, Australia, even China – I have heard that he travels about the world, stopping wherever he can find work. Where he is now nobody knows. Your mama was always sorry that we never reconciled, but sometimes stories do not have happy endings. Take this as a lesson, Fanny and Theodore. Always get along. Do not let ambition poison the natural affection you have for one another. Now it is late."

He leaned over and kissed my forehead. "Tomorrow we must continue preparing the next magician in the family. Right, Theodore?"

Listening, I heard the gentle sound of Theodore snoring. He had already fallen asleep. My father sighed and went out.

✳ 4 ✳

THE NOT VERY MIRACULOUS CATCH

The day before the opening of the show arrived. The theater front was festooned with the new poster that showed the Great Zandini commanding his son to rise out of a giant egg. I was in the poster too, but only in the background, peaking out of a wicker basket and wearing a turban on my head. It seemed to me that the artist had done almost too good a job. Rather than pleased, Theodore looked as dismayed on the poster as he did in real life.

But I couldn't help being tremendously excited. A crowd of admirers, as well as journalists from the Paris newspapers, gathered outside the theater and chanted for Father to make an appearance. Carriages stopped, blocking the street. Finally we came out and Father stood on a trunk to address them.

"Dear friends," he called. "Tomorrow is a very special day. Not only is it the start of a new show, but it is also the beginning of my son's glorious career on the stage. He will conquer Paris, not by the sword but by magic!"

At these last words Father waved his cane, and rose petals descended on the crowd. Everyone cheered. I looked at Theodore beside me and saw that he was staring angrily at someone in the throng before us.

"Theodore, who are you looking at?" I asked.

"Him! A. S. Besette, the reporter who writes those nasty things. See him?"

I looked and saw a rather short and rotund man with a very dark beard, a cigar stuck in his mouth, and a monocle in his eye. He was writing in a little pad, a smile on his face that was more like a sneer.

"Don't worry about that scribbler," I said. "Just concentrate on the performance tomorrow."

But the next morning the Paris *Gazette* carried a front-page story.

ALL PARIS AWAITS ZANDINI OPENING

BY A. S. BESETTE, CONJURING REPORTER

As just about everyone in the city of lights knows, tonight is the first performance of the new show by the Great Zandini. Yesterday the conjurer presented his son to a small group of admirers. Rather than having his father's forceful presence, young Theodore seemed to shrink before the attention. No doubt he is feeling the enormous pressure of having to perform on stage for the first time. Will he succeed? Read this newspaper tomorrow to find out.

"'Small group'!" Father sputtered. "Theodore, tonight we'll show that Besette whether or not you've inherited the Zandini talent."

Tickets for the first performance sold out quickly. Even the mayor of Paris and his wife planned to attend. Two hours before show time we arrived at the theater to make sure that all the equipment was in order. Before the curtain went up, my father took my brother's hand and mine. "Dear children," he said, and I saw a tear shining in his eye. "If only your mother could see you tonight. I know you will make me proud."

The house lights dimmed, the orchestra began to play a mysterious and powerful melody, and slowly the curtain rose to an exotic interior of eastern rugs, strangely carved furniture, and luxurious tapestries. Then a flash of smoke and, to the amazement of the audience, the Great Zandini stood before them. He bowed to the applause, and as I watched from the wings, I thought that he had never looked so handsome.

In the show Father turned scarves from yellow to blue to red. He caused an empty bowl to fill with water, poured the water out, and caused it to magically fill again. He swallowed a small bell and then shook his right hand so that the bell rang inside him, then jiggled the bell through his body so that it rang when he shook his left foot.

He fried eggs upon a sheet of writing paper. He swallowed twenty sewing needles one at a time, then a long thread, and finally drew the thread out of his mouth with the needles all threaded upon it.

He hypnotized me and commanded me to rise in the air.

He brought a wooden model of Noah's Ark on stage, lowering all four sides to show that it was empty. He filled it with water and then, from a small window, pulled out ducks, chickens, cats, snakes, and even a pig.

Finally he wheeled out a giant cage, covered it with a silk cloth, and pulled off the cloth to reveal a snarling lion. Suddenly the lion burst out of the cage, causing the audience to scream. But just as the people were about to flee in terror, the lion halted and with its huge paws pulled off its own head to reveal Father inside.

Each illusion had been more brilliant than the last. Standing up with the lion head under his arm, Father stepped forward to speak to the audience. "Ladies and gentlemen, I wish to present, for the first time on stage, Theodore, Son of the Great Zandini. He will perform a marvelous illusion called the Miraculous Catch."

Theodore stood beside me in the wings. "I don't want to go," he whispered.

"You show them," I said, giving him a shove. He practically flew onto the stage. His face looked a ghastly shade of green. Only now, peering out, did I notice in the front row none other than A. S. Besette with his note pad. Theodore took the fishing rod from Father, shuffled toward the foot of the stage, and then cast the fishing line over the heads of the audience. He was supposed to catch a fish magically out of the air, a trick we had rehearsed countless times. But instead of the fish, Theodore hooked the wig of the mayor's wife. The wig flew up from her head.

The mayor's wife screamed. The mayor shouted. The audience laughed and jeered.

Theodore tried to lower the wig back onto her head, but instead it landed on the bald head of the mayor.

"Oh dear," Theodore said. And then he giggled.

Sure enough, the next morning an article appeared on the *Gazette's* front page.

SON OF ZANDINI CATCHES RARE HAIRY FISH

BY A. S. BESETTE, CONJURING REPORTER

If you were at the Theater Zandini last night then you too are hoping that the wife of our mayor has recovered from the shock. Unless the Son of the Great Zandini was trying to catch a hairy fish previously unknown to exist, we can only conclude that he bungled his one trick. Perhaps Theodore should start fishing for a new line of work.

"It is my fault," Father consoled Theo over breakfast. "The Miraculous Catch is a difficult illusion. You were not ready. Tonight we will try something else. Just remember, the true performer takes a failure as a challenge. This evening, you will win them over!"

All morning I helped Theodore to practice the Astounding Mind Reading Act. I said, "Papa's right. You have to show them that you really are the son of a great magician. If I were you, Theodore, I couldn't wait to get on the stage again. And I would be so tremendous that the audience would have to love me!"

"But Fanny," Theodore said, "I don't care if they love me. The only one I care about is Colette." Then he began to hum and pretend that he was dancing, no doubt imagining Colette in his arms.

Father soon discovered that almost everyone in Paris had read A. S. Besette's article. Only half the tickets had sold for the evening show. I knew that I had to do something to help, but what?

I was alone in the apartment. Papa had gone to the theater, while Theodore was receiving sympathy from Colette. I paced about, trying to come up with a plan. In the dining room I stared hard at the family portraits, first of Mother, and then Great-grandfather, Grandfather, Father, and finally at Uncle Zachariah. He looked like my father, only he was clean shaven and his eyes were different – hard and gleaming. I thought that if anyone might inspire me it was my resentful, scheming uncle, and I stared for a long time into those eyes. I almost felt as if he was looking back at me.

And then I had it.

Of course I knew that if Father found out his pride would be hurt, and so I would have to keep it a secret. Quickly I looked through the closet until I found a trunk of Theodore's old clothes. I put on a tweed jacket, short pants, stockings, and even a pair of scuffed shoes. I tucked my hair into a cap. Then I gazed at myself in the mirror. Not bad, I thought, but my face still looked too much like a girl's. I took some coal dust from the grate and smudged it on my cheeks. Better.

Of course, just looking like a boy wasn't enough. I tried clomping my feet, shrugging my shoulders, sticking my hands in my pockets, curling my lip – everything I thought boys did. Then I practiced speaking in a lower voice out of the corner of my mouth.

Ready or not, I was running out of time. I went out into the streets of Paris.

* 5 *

HOW TO BAKE A CAKE

Come and see the Great Zandini!" I called out, making sure to keep my voice low. "Witness the most spectacular illusions! And for the first time ever, see his son, inheritor of the Great Zandini's magic secrets! Tonight at the Theater Zandini!"

And so I walked, past the glittering shops and through the squares. As they listened, I saw people grin and whisper to one another. No doubt they too had read A. S. Besette's newspaper article and were making fun of Father and Theodore. How fickle people are! One moment they are cheering for you and the next they are laughing at you. Still, I called out until my throat became sore and my feet throbbed from walking.

I came to the great Central Food Market of Paris, the place where cartloads of fresh fish and oysters, vegetables and fruit, butter and cheese, and everything else there is to eat arrive at dawn each morning. "Come and see the Great Zandini and his son!" I cried.

A man in a bowler hat had just bought a carnation from a flower seller and was putting it into the buttonhole of his lapel. He laughed and said in a loud voice, "Are you sure that it's a conjuring show? From what I've read it sounds more like a clown act."

Anger grew like a hot flame inside me. "You doubt the Great Zandini, sir? Then let me demonstrate something that he taught me. Would you be so kind as to lend me your hat?"

"But it's brand new."

People stopped to listen. "All the better," I said, taking it from him. "Now, dear Madame Egg Seller, would you kindly lend me two eggs?"

The woman gave me the eggs. "Now you're in for it!" she chuckled. A circle of people had formed around us, pointing and talking. I cracked each egg and dropped the gooey contents right into the hat.

"You're ruining it!" the man moaned.

"I certainly hope I remember how to do this." I scratched my head and pondered. "Oh yes, now I need two cups of flour."

"Coming right up!" said the man who ran the flour stall. I took the flour and dumped it into the hat.

"Surely you need milk!" said the milk merchant.

"And sugar!"

"And butter!"

All of it went – *plop!* – into the hat.

"Well?" the man asked nervously.

I gazed down into the hat. I pouted.

"I knew it!" the man fumed. "You are going to have to pay for my hat."

"I know what the problem is," I said. I've forgotten to say the magic words." And waving my hand over the hat, I closed my eyes and recited a rhyme.

> *Whether a hat is old or new,*
> *it's as good as any pan,*
> *and those who doubt the Great Zandini*
> *will look as foolish as this man!*

At that I put my hand into the hat and pulled out a three-layer cake with chocolate icing.

The crowd laughed and applauded. The man's face turned a deep violet. "Would you care for a piece?" I asked him. From a vendor I borrowed a knife. When I cut the cake a dove flew into the sky.

"Ah!" said the crowd.

"Remember," I called out. "See the Great Zandini and his son! Eight o'clock at the Theater Zandini."

The crowd rushed to the theater. As I followed behind I saw them tell their friends and neighbors and even strangers, so that soon the show was sold out.

"You see?" Father said, peeking out through the curtain just before the performance. I had been careful to get home before anyone else, wash my face, and change back into my dress. "A bad review cannot harm the reputation of the Great Zandini," Father went on. "Theodore, here is your chance."

Once again Father performed splendidly. And again near the end of the show, he made an announcement. "Tonight, ladies and gentlemen, Theodore, Son of the Great Zandini, will demonstrate his remarkable ability to read minds."

Theodore looked no happier than the night before as he came onto the stage. Father tied a blindfold over his eyes. "I will now go into the audience," he said. "Please feel free to offer me any object that you like. My son will be able to read your mind and tell us what the object is."

Father leapt gracefully from the stage and began to walk up the aisle. A man handed over a wallet and Father held it up. "A useful item," Father said. "And I'd bet good money you can divine what it is, Theodore."

Theodore said, "Is it a shoe?"

Father cleared his throat. "Concentrate son. Let's try something else." A woman gave him a necklace of pearls. "Can you read the lady's mind, Theo? If you do it will be as amazing as – as a gift from the sea!"

Theodore rubbed his head with one hand. I think I have it," he said. "It's a flounder!"

Father pretended to laugh. "Very amusing. Let's have one last try. Does someone have an interesting object to lend?"

A man gave father a pocket watch. "Ah," said Father. "It's about time you read this gentleman's mind, Theodore."

My brother furrowed his brow. He thought. He thought some more. "I know!" he cried. "It's a hot water bottle! No? A small dog! Wrong? How about a bicycle?"

The audience threw fruit and vegetables at the stage. Father scrambled back in a rather undignified hurry. A ripe plum hit Theodore on the side of his head, but he couldn't see it because of the blindfold. He touched the dripping plum with a finger and put the finger into his mouth. It was strange how relieved he looked now that the trick was over, even if he had failed.

The curtain came thumping down.

✳ 6 ✳

A VISIT TO
A. S. BESETTE

Each evening a new disaster occurred. One night Theodore bungled an escape act, trapping himself in a barrel. On another he levitated me four feet into the air, only to drop me on my behind. Every day I had to rush about the city performing so that the seats that night would not all be empty.

One afternoon I put on my boy's disguise and performed in the Luxembourg Gardens. After sprinkling a few seeds into a pot, I commanded a tree to grow instantly. From the tree sprouted real oranges, which I then handed out to the delighted onlookers. From among the crowd a man's hand thrust out to take one of the oranges. The hand had an exquisite manicure and wore a large gold ring on the pinky finger. Looking up, I saw a big beard and unsmiling mouth beneath a silk hat. A dark eye peered at me through a monocle. Instantly I knew that this was A. S. Besette, conjuring reporter of the Paris *Gazette*.

A. S. Besette said, "Neatly done, young man." Before I could reply, the others had crowded about and he was gone.

But sure enough, the next morning there was an article in the newspaper, which my father read aloud to us at the breakfast table.

A NEW TALENT

BY A. S. BESETTE, CONJURING REPORTER

All of Paris is talking about the mysterious young magician who astonished passersby in the Luxembourg Gardens yesterday. Who is this boy who can make trees grow at his command? Not only is he skilled at magic, but he is a natural performer who clearly loves to entertain and make people laugh, smile, and gasp in amazement. Dear readers, I advise you to keep a look out for this fascinating young gentleman. In this humble reporter's opinion, he is giving the best show in town.

"What's this?" Father said with a scowl. "Someone trying to upstage the Great Zandini?"

"Oh surely not, Father," I replied. "No doubt he is just some street performer earning a little money."

"Well, that's a nice trick he pulled off. I used to perform something like it myself."

When I dared to look up I saw Theodore staring at me.

Poor Theodore did not improve. Father and I spent a whole week practicing the Floating Ball with him until we felt sure he was ready. During the show he came out wearing an elaborate oriental robe. He commanded a large silver ball to rise from the stage and float about the air. The audience clapped warmly, but suddenly the ball began to tremble. Theodore looked up in dismay. The ball swung from side to side, seemed to bounce in the air, and then dropped to the stage floor, shattering into a thousand pieces.

Each new catastrophe appeared the next morning in the Paris *Gazette*. Meanwhile, A. S. Besette kept praising "the mysterious young magician." One afternoon, sneaking back into the apartment after several hours of street performing, I was about to change out of my disguise when Theodore suddenly leapt from out of the closet, frightening me half to death.

"Fanny! I knew it was you," he said. "After all, I've seen you practice that orange tree trick a hundred times. But are you mad? If Father finds out, he'll – well, I don't know what he'll do."

"I'm only trying to help."

"Are you sure about that? Maybe you like the attention. It isn't Father's fault that A. S. Besette is writing such nasty things about our show. It's mine. And now some new magician comes along and gets praised to the skies. Father's feelings are going to be hurt. Maybe even worse if he finds out that the magician making our show look bad is you."

"Then we have to make sure he doesn't find out," I said.

"That's not going to be easy, not if Besette keeps writing about you. Sooner or later he's bound to figure out who you are."

"I hadn't thought about that," I said. Maybe Theodore was right. Maybe I was too busy enjoying A. S. Besette's praise of me even if I did hate what he wrote about Father and Theo. "All right," I said, heading back to the door. "I'm going to do something about it."

"What?"

"You'll see."

I knew that the offices of the *Gazette* were in a run-down old building near the big cemetery. Still dressed as a boy, I took a tram to get there. The front office was bustling with reporters and messengers running in and out, bells ringing, editors shouting orders. I asked the man at the front desk if I could see Monsieur Besette.

The man eyed me suspiciously. "He's a very busy reporter. Why do you want to see him?"

"Tell him that the mysterious young magician is here."

The man's eyebrow went up. "Wait here."

Two minutes later I was standing in A. S. Besette's office, the reporter sitting behind his desk. While it was covered with papers and pens and blots of ink, he wasn't writing but flipping a coin in the air. He caught the coin and then, smiling, opened his hand to show me that it had disappeared.

"I see you are an amateur magician, Monsieur," I said, careful to speak in my boy's voice. "Unfortunately, I saw you drop it into your sleeve. Perhaps you need to practice more."

He made a sour face and then brusquely scratched his beard.

"So you have come to see me," he said. "And what can I do for you, young man?"

"I want you to stop writing about me."

"How unusual, a performer who does not like praise."

"And also to stop saying those mean things about the Great Zandini. He's the world's best magician."

"So some believe. But I don't think anyone would say that his son is the second best. It appears that he takes after his Uncle Zachariah after all."

"What do you know about the Great Zandini's brother?"

"I saw him perform many years before your time. In fact, I was present in the theater on the night he disappeared. You see, young man, I felt that I understood Zachariah. I too am an older brother and I know what it feels like to have a younger sibling get all the attention."

"So that is why you became a critic of conjurers? To make others feel bad?"

"Not at all. I became a critic because I can tell a good magician from a poor one. And I'm sorry to say that the Great Zandini's son falls into the second category."

I felt my temper rising at the remark against Theo, but what could I do? After all, I could hardly expect A. S. Besette to lie about my brother's performances. "There's an old saying," I said finally. "If you can't say something nice then don't say anything at all."

"That doesn't apply to newspaper reporters."

"What do you have against, against –" I had almost said my father, "– against the Great Zandini? And his son? It isn't right not to give a person a fair chance."

I looked straight into his eyes. A. S. Besette stared back for a moment but then he looked away. "I'll think about it," he said.

"Thank you, Monsieur," I said, and making a little bow I backed out of his office.

✳ 7 ✳

A CHALLENGE
IS OFFERED

But the reporter did not keep his word. Two days later Father read aloud another item from the newspaper.

JUST WHO IS
THE GREATEST?

BY A. S. BESETTE, CONJURING REPORTER

The mysterious young magician continues to baffle people all over the city. Just yesterday patrons of the Café Voltaire gasped as they watched him take up a single glass bottle and from it pour coffee, then milk, beer, lemonade, and finally hot chocolate. Meanwhile, the Great Zandini and his son have become the laughing stock of Paris. Therefore, this humble reporter asks the question, just who really is the greatest magician?

―――――――――――――――――――――――

"What's this?" Father raged. "The Great Zandini compared to a mere sidewalk hustler! This cannot go on. That young rascal has to be taught a lesson. And so does Besette. It is time they found out just who is the best. But what can I do? What?"

We watched Father pace rapidly back and forth. Theodore shot me a look, as if to say, "See what you've done?" Suddenly Father halted, slapping his hands together. "I have it! I will issue a challenge – a duel of magical skill between the young magician and me."

"But Papa," Theodore said quickly, "I'm sure the young magician would never dare show up. Right, Fanny?" He kicked me under the table.

"Ouch!" I cried. And then, "I mean, no, never," as I rubbed the sore spot on my leg.

That very afternoon Father asked us to come out with him, but Theodore had a date with Colette. And so I went in the carriage to the offices of the Paris *Gazette*. On this visit, though, I was my girl self, with a ribbon in my hair and a pale yellow dress, and the desk clerk did not recognize me. He did, however, recognize Father.

"Monsieur Zandini!" he exclaimed.

"Let me see that pen-scratcher who works here. Besette."

"Just one moment."

The clerk scrambled from his chair. A moment later we were being ushered into A. S. Besette's office. When the reporter looked up he did not even glance at me but stared at my father, first in surprise and then dismay. He half rose out of his chair, his mouth moving as if he were trying to speak but could find no words.

"Zandini!" he said at last, as if he could not believe it. His monocle dropped out of his eye.

"Yes, it is I, Zandini," said my father. "And this is for you." He tossed a sheet of paper onto the desk. "Put this in your newspaper. Then we will see who is the laughing stock of Paris. Come along, Fanny."

He turned around again and marched out. I saw A. S. Besette put in his monocle again and stare at Father with a pained look. Did he feel a twinge of regret for all those mean things he had written? Then I too ran out.

Sure enough, a notice appeared on the front page of the evening edition.

A CHALLENGE TO THE MYSTERIOUS YOUNG MAGICIAN

BY A. S. BESETTE, CONJURING REPORTER

This humble reporter was most surprised to see none other than the Great Zandini in his office this very afternoon. Did the celebrated conjurer appear in a flash of lightning? Or materialize out of a medicine bottle? No, he merely walked

through the door. His purpose was to deliver the
following notice:

*The Great Zandini announces that tomorrow, at five
o'clock in the afternoon, he will be standing beneath the
city's latest landmark, the Eiffel Tower. He hopes that
the mysterious young magician has the courage to meet
him there for a contest of conjuring skill. All interested
members of the public are invited to attend.*

No doubt fans of the magical arts will make their way
to the tower to witness this once-in-a-lifetime
showdown. This reporter certainly wouldn't miss it!

Father read the article with a smile of satisfaction. I, however, felt
rather different emotions. What was I to do? How could I go against
my own father in a contest?

By the next morning, all of Paris was talking about the challenge.
In the patisseries, the dressmakers' shops, and the artists' studios,
people spoke of nothing else. Arguments broke out as to who was
the greater magician, sometimes becoming so heated that the gen-
darmes had to be called to separate the antagonists. New fashions
swept over the city as men carried magic wands instead of walking
sticks and women wore hats decorated with playing cards. On street
corners musicians played *The Conjurer's Waltz* on their accordions

while poets stood on tables in the cafés and recited poems about Father and his rival.

I had hardly expected so much hoopla and while I had to admit that it was terrifically exciting, it was also frightening. Should I accept the challenge? A decision just seemed impossible to make.

An hour before the contest, I was sitting on my bed when Theodore came into my room. He closed the door behind him.

"Well?" he said in a whisper. "What are you going to do?"

"I don't know yet."

"Then I'll tell you, Fanny. Don't show up. You can't duel with Father in front of all of Paris. It just wouldn't be right. And what if you win? After all, Father is getting older. If you're not careful, Fanny, you will split the family just as Uncle Zachariah once did. Make up some excuse and stay home. And that will be the end of the mysterious young magician."

Theo went out again. When I too came out of my room, Father was dressed in the suit and hat he wore for performances. "Hurry up, Fanny," he said when he saw that I was not ready. "Do you want to be the only person in Paris not to see your father prove that he is the world's finest magician?" Then he frowned and came over to put his cool hand on my forehead. "What is the matter? Don't you feel well?"

"It's just a headache, Papa. You go ahead of me. I promise to catch up."

"Are you sure?"

"Yes, I'll be fine."

And so Father and Theodore left. I went to the sofa and made myself lie down. Each minute that ticked by on the mantel clock seemed like an eternity. Suddenly I heard a voice calling up from the street.

It was Colette. I hurried down the apartment stairs to find her in the doorway. She wore a beautiful taffeta dress with matching blue ribbons in her hair. "Good afternoon, Fanny," she said. "My family is waiting in a carriage to go watch your father and that young magician. I just wanted to wish the Great Zandini luck."

"He has already gone," I said. "And so has Theodore."

"Oh, I see." She turned to go but then hesitated and turned back again. "Are you all right, Fanny?" she said.

Colette looked at me. Had Theodore told her that I was the mysterious young magician? I felt sure that he kept no secrets from her. "I don't know what to do," I said.

She smiled gently. "But you do."

"I do?"

"Yes," Colette said. "From all that Theodore has told me about you, I'm sure that you do know what to do. You are just not listening carefully enough to yourself. But if you listen, you'll know." Then she curtsied and left.

Slowly I closed the door. What did she mean? I already knew what to do and only had to listen to myself? Well, it seemed to me that I had nothing to lose by trying, and so I stood very still and closed my eyes. For a moment I could hear a confusion of voices in my head – Father, Theodore, A. S. Besette, even Colette – all talking at once. But after a few moments they grew silent one by one.

And then, yes, I heard my own. Colette was right. I *did* know what to do.

I ran back up to the apartment and pulled out my boy's disguise of jacket, short pants, stockings, and cap. Quickly I dressed, smudged my face with coal dust, and then prepared myself for the magic that I would have to perform. I flew out of the apartment, crossed the bridge to the Left Bank, and ran along the quay by the river.

✳ 8 ✳

THE RIVALS MEET

By the time I got to the base of the Eiffel Tower a huge crowd had gathered beneath its four gigantic iron legs. People stood on top of the new motor cars and climbed lampposts in order to get a better view. They waved flags and blew horns.

I squeezed my way through until I reached the front, where I could see Father waving his top hat. I could also see Theodore standing beside Colette and, on the other side of the crowd, A. S. Besette, who was polishing his monocle with a handkerchief.

"Dear friends," Father called out. "I am most gratified to see you all here. I had hoped to show you a demonstration of the finest conjuring skills this afternoon, but alas it appears that the young upstart has decided not to show up. No doubt he is too afraid to meet me."

Too afraid! Hearing those words, I could not keep quiet, even if it was my own father who had said them.

"But you are wrong!" I called in a loud voice.

The crowd parted to let me through. Immediately I stepped into the circle to face Father.

"So here you are at last," he said.

"How could I miss a chance to meet the Great Zandini?" I said. "But what is that in your ear?"

Reaching toward him, I pulled out a fork, a knife, and a spoon. The spectators applauded.

"But you have something in your ear too," the Great Zandini said. He drew out an umbrella! Even I had never seen him do that before. The applause grew louder.

"See what is beneath your jacket." He reached in and drew out a birdcage. Inside was a parrot, with the most beautiful plumage, that immediately began to whistle *The Conjurer's Waltz*.

And so we continued. I pulled out a flute from beneath his coat, which then began to play by itself; he found a mandolin under my jacket. I produced a glass of wine from inside his hat; he drew a bottle of champagne from my cap. Bouquets of flowers, several fans, a woman's corset, a telescope, a pair of men's long underwear, two rabbits, a large clock, a porcelain doll, a mirror, a shaving mug, dumbbells, and a pair of ice-skates – soon the ground was littered all around us. Whatever I produced, Father found something better. Both of us were exhausted. Finally the Great Zandini stretched out his hand. "See what's in your mouth!" he said. And from between my lips he drew an egg; then a second, and a third. He threw them into the air where they exploded with a shower of red, blue, and white fireworks – the colors of France. Great cheers from the crowd.

I had no more tricks left; Father had won. I felt both glad and disappointed. Father said, "I must concede that you are the finest young conjurer I have ever seen. Who was your teacher?"

"No less than the world's greatest magician," I answered. Suddenly I had an inspiration. "And he taught me one last trick."

"What is that?"

"I can turn myself into your daughter."

"Into Fanny? But how?"

"Like this," I said, taking off my cap and shaking loose my hair.

We stood looking at one another a moment, and then my father threw his arms around me. People tossed their hats in the air and shouted, "Bravo, Great Zandini! Bravo, Daughter of the Great Zandini!" When Father and I let go of one another I saw that Theodore was cheering more loudly than anyone. Beside him, Colette was smiling and blushing. But what was truly strange was that when I looked over at A. S. Besette, I saw that he was pretending to blow his nose with his handkerchief to hide the tears in his eyes.

"Wait," Father said. "I too have one last trick."

The crowd grew quiet again. He took three quick strides across the circle. "I can turn Monsieur Besette into your uncle." In one swift movement he pulled A. S. Besette's beard, which came away from his face. It was false! The reporter blushed in embarrassment.

"Uncle Zachariah!" I said in amazement. "Is it really you?"

"Yes," said A. S. Besette, or rather Uncle Zachariah. "Will you forgive me?"

✳ 9 ✳

ZANDINI AND DAUGHTER

But how did you know?" I asked Father, after all the excitement had died down. We were back at the apartment where Matilda had prepared for us – even Uncle Zachariah – a celebratory dinner. "You haven't seen Uncle Zachariah in so long. And he wore a beard. And he's grown so stout!"

"Stout!" Uncle laughed. "But I too wish to know, dear brother."

"In truth, I did not know until the last moment when I saw you crying. Your eyes have not changed, Zachariah, and you looked just the same as when you used to cry as a boy."

"Yes, I was always the emotional one in the family. Anger, tears – from one to another, I'm afraid. It really is very good of you to forgive me for all the things I've written and for hiding these long years."

"I don't have any choice, Zachariah. My dear wife made me promise that, one day, you and I would be reconciled. But don't think I'll ever forget some of those things you wrote!"

"They did make you a better magician, didn't they?" Theodore said. "Those articles always spurred you on to work harder."

"Perhaps," Father grumbled.

"Papa," I said, helping myself to seconds of everything, for I found myself ravenously hungry. "Did you really not suspect that I was the mysterious young magician?"

"I should have known, Fanny. After all, you learned your magic from me, and I ought to have recognized that Zandini style. I suppose I just did not open my own eyes to how good you are."

"What time is it?" cried Uncle Zachariah, wiping his mouth with a napkin. "I've got to hurry if I'm to make the deadline for the morning edition."

"Don't tell me you're still going to be a reporter," Father said.

"Of course I am. I found something that I'm good at, and I might as well stick to it. You don't want me to become a magician again, do you?"

"No!" said Father, Theodore, and I all at once.

The next morning we eagerly turned to the front page of the Paris *Gazette*.

ZANDINIS TRIUMPH

BY A. S. BESETTE, CONJURING REPORTER

Have the citizens of Paris ever been so amazed, so amused, so astounded? The revelation that the mysterious young magician is none other than the Great Zandini's own daughter will surely be remembered for years to come. And it proves without a doubt that the Zandinis are the greatest conjuring family of all time. As for this humble reporter, the revealing of his true identity as Zachariah Zander, long-lost brother of the Great Zandini, only added to the extraordinary proceedings. He wishes to publicly apologize for his jealous grudge against his talented brother and hopes that the kind readers will excuse his deception.

As for what happens next, Parisians will just have to buy a ticket to tonight's performance and find out for themselves.

We all thought it was good of Uncle Zachariah to promote the evening's performance, and indeed the theater was swarmed with people trying to buy tickets. That evening my father performed more magnificently than ever before. He hypnotized me and suspended me horizontally in the air, with only my elbow resting on the top of a walking stick. He asked for two men in the audience to tie him securely with ropes to a chair and lock him in a cabinet along with a guitar, a flute, several horns, as well as a stack of dishes and cups. As soon as the cabinet was closed, the instruments began to play and the cups and plates to fly out of the open top and crash upon the stage. But when the men quickly opened the cabinet, Father was still securely tied.

Finally, Father made an announcement.

"Ladies and gentlemen, I take great pleasure in presenting for the first time under her own name the Amazing Fanny, Daughter of the Great Zandini!"

Listening to the applause, I trembled with nervousness and excitement. Theodore patted me on the shoulder. "Just remember to enjoy yourself," he smiled, and I smiled back at him. On stage, I performed the Floating Ball without a fault. Then the Miraculous Catch, snatching three fish out of the air and dropping them each into a bowl of water. For the finale, Father blindfolded me, and I correctly divined every object that he held up. As my father and I took our bows, the audience stood up and cheered.

From then on we were the toast of Paris. Every night the theater sold out, and at the end of each performance the stage was strewn with roses.

On Sunday, Uncle Zachariah accompanied us on a carriage ride through the Bois de Boulogne. People raised their hats to us. "All right, Fanny," Father said with a smile. "You have certainly proved that a father does not always know what is best. When I retire you will become the next Great Zandini, continuing the family tradition. That is, if you wish to."

"Oh yes, Papa."

"And Theodore, you may marry Colette, when you come of age, and open your phonograph shop. Especially since your sister's encouragement will no doubt convince you to do so anyway."

"I'm so glad, Papa."

"But Papa," I said. "You are not so very old. Can't we go on performing together for a while yet?"

"Fanny's right," Uncle Zachariah said. "You've still got a few good tricks up your sleeve."

And so that was just what we did. The Great Zandini and daughter, performing each night, astonishing audiences by making the impossible seem possible.